FOR SCOTT AND LETA, AND CROCODILES EVERYWHERE —ES
FOR DAD — JM

Tundra Books, an imprint of Penguin Random House Canada Young Readers,
a division of Penguin Random House of Canada Limited

Library and Archives Canada Cataloguing in Publication

Title: Crocodile hungry / written by Eija Sumner ; illustrated by John Martz.
Names: Sumner, Eija, author. | Martz, John, 1978- illustrator.
Identifiers: Canadiana (print) 20200410954 | Canadiana (ebook) 20200410962
ISBN 9780735267879 (hardcover) | ISBN 9780735267886 (EPUB)
Classification: LCC PZ7.1.S943 Cr 2022 | DDC j813/.6—dc23

Published simultaneously in the United States of America by Tundra Books of Northern
New York, an imprint of Penguin Random House Canada Young Readers,
a division of Penguin Random House of Canada Limited

Library of Congress Control Number: 2020951320

Edited by Samantha Swenson
Designed by John Martz
The artwork in this book was created with ink, paper and a computer.
The type was drawn by hand.

Printed in China

www.penguinrandomhouse.ca

1   2   3   4   5   26   25   24   23   22

Penguin
Random House
tundra   TUNDRA BOOKS

CROCODILE HUNGRY

WRITTEN BY EIJA SUMNER

ILLUSTRATED BY JOHN MARTZ

tundra

CANNED HAM?
TOO HARD TO OPEN.

BEEF JERKY?
GETS STUCK IN TEETH.

EGGS?
BITE SHELL,
GET TOOTHACHE.

CROCODILE
KNOWS.

GO TO
FARMERS'
MARKET.

GROCERY STORE?

COMMUNITY GARDEN?

CROCODILE NOT LIKE
LETTUCE ANYWAY.

CROCODILE SO HUNGRY.
STARTING TO GET **HANGRY!**

CROCODILE.
WANTS.
FOOD.
NOW.

CROCODILE'S TUMMY GRUMBLES.

CROCODILE SO TIRED BEING HUNGRY.
CROCODILE SAD NOW.

CROCODILE CRIES.

CROCODILE CRIES CROCODILE TEARS.

CROCODILE TEARS FOR DAYS.
WEEKS.

CROCODILE SURROUNDED BY
NICE-SIZED POND NOW.

BIRDS VISIT.
PRETTY PINK BIRDS.
FLAMINGO BIRDS.

CROCODILE'S TUMMY RUMBLES.

NO SUMMER SAUSAGE IN POND.
NO BACON OR BOLOGNA.
NO LAMB CHOPS OR LINGUIÇA.

ONLY PINK MARSHMALLOW BIRDS ON STILTS.

WHAT CAN CROCODILE EAT?

CROCODILE
KNOWS.